A CHRISTMAS *Escape*

A Novella

—SMALL TOWN CHRISTMAS—
BOOK 7

❅ ❅ ❅

D. ALLEN

DN Publishing

A Christmas Escape

Small Town Christmas, Book 7

Copyright © 2022 by D. Allen

Batavia, NY

www.DavidNethBooks.com

ISBN: 978-1-945336-31-7
First Edition

Subscribe to the author's newsletter for updates and exclusive content:
DavidNethBooks.com/Newsletter

Follow the author at:
www.facebook.com/DavidNethBooks
www.instagram.com/DavidNethBooks

Also by D. Allen

<u>Montana Beach</u>
Summer Stay

Summer Job

Summer Nights

<u>Small Town Christmas</u>
A Christmas Reunion

A Christmas Charade

A Christmas Spark

A Christmas Song

A Christmas Departure

A Christmas Wedding

A Christmas Escape

<u>Standalone</u>
Snow After Christmas

DECEMBER 16TH
Steph

* * *

"What are you doing for the holidays?" I ask my friend Lisa in the staff room at work.

Around the small room, there are other DesignUP Developers employees, but it's only me and Lisa at our table. We're also the only two currently in the staff room from the Planning and Development department.

"Going back home," Lisa says with a smile. She pulls out a baggie of carrots and a small Tupperware container with peanut butter. "But Jim and I are not staying with my parents." Lisa grew up in Canandaigua, only about a thirty minute drive from Rochester.

"You don't want to stay with your husband in your old childhood bedroom?" I tease.

Lisa scoffs. "God no. We're getting an Airbnb to stay in. It's a loft apartment in one of the old commercial buildings on Main Street. The pictures look really cute."

Spreading out my lunch on the plastic red table cloth someone had put on each table, I say, "I'm sure your parents are thrilled about that." I pull out my PB&J sandwich. I might be thirty-two, but the grade school go-to is still a favorite.

Lisa shakes her head as she chomps down on her carrot. "The house will be insane. My brother and his wife are coming in and staying with them. And my sister is coming with her two kids. So unless Jim and I wanted to sleep on the dank pull-out in the basement, we kind of have no other choice." She dipped her next carrot in her peanut butter and waved it at me. "Don't get me wrong. I love the crazy. But I also need my own room to escape to."

I nod. "Understandable. So you just hang out at your parents' for Christmas then?"

"Well, on Christmas Day, yeah. But we're going up a few days before to really soak in the season."

I scrunch my brow. "What does that mean?"

"You know: shopping up and down Main Street, visiting Sonnenberg Gardens with my niece and nephew just like we used to do when we were younger, catching up with old friends." She shrugs. "Reconnecting with my small town roots. It's beautifully simple there. Everything seems to click back into place for me, you know?"

Shaking my head, I say, "I guess I've never really had that feeling."

There's an awkward silence as the two of us continue with our lunch. I admire the Christmas tree in the corner. The company's efforts to bring holiday cheer and boost morale as we close out the year and everyone starts to wind down for the season. Can't say it really fuels me to keep working, but I still enjoy the warmth it brings.

The boisterous conversations coming from the other tables only seems to point out just how quiet Lisa and I have become.

"So are you going back to Maine for the holidays?" Lisa suddenly asks.

"No. It's my brother's turn to have my parents for Christmas, so they're flying to Seattle to see his family."

"And you're not joining them?"

Tossing my trash in my lunch bag, I shake my head. "That's a little over my budget this year."

"Do you have any friends you're going to hang out with then?"

"Not really," I say. "Most of the people I know in Rochester have plans already and I don't want to intrude."

"Oh, well I'd invite you along to stay with us, but I think Jim is extra-excited to have a place to ourselves. If I'm being perfectly honest, one of my gifts to him is that I'm finally off the pill."

My eyes widen at the revelation of something so personal. "Oh."

"Yeah, we've been married five years, getting into our mid-thirties. I think it's time to finally start that family we've been talking about. Knowing my husband, he'll want to get started *right away*, which means we need some alone time."

"Right," I say with a nod. This conversation took an awkward turn. Quickly, I downplay the sympathy I know is coming. "I'll be okay. Really. It'll be nice to have a low-key holiday. I'll Zoom with my family, watch some movies, play some music. Certainly, I'll be gorging myself in Christmas cookies regardless of who is or isn't there."

Lisa politely laughs along with me. "Well, that's good that you have a plan."

"Yeah. I'll be okay on my own." I fold up my brown paper lunch bag that contains my trash as tightly as possible. "Honestly, I have enough time to take off now through the end of the year, but I'm holding off. Why indulge in my holiday plans early and then be bored on Christmas?"

"You should take the time if you have it!" Lisa encourages. "Relax and be well-rested before the New Year."

I turn away and start to get up. "Yeah, yeah, yeah. We'll see. I have some projects to finish up here before I take any time off."

"You'll never take time if you wait for the right time. That's the same way I feel about starting a family. We need to just do it and make it work."

As we exit the break room, Lisa continues to talk about the possibility of her having a baby by next Christmas. Meanwhile, I can't help but notice just how different our lives are.

DECEMBER 16TH
Steph

❄ ❄ ❄

Later that day, I find myself in Monica's office. She's the manager of our department. The one who sits in on the meetings with the big-whigs and doles out the orders to our department straight from the big guys.

Our company isn't huge, but it's large enough to have scaffolded levels of management. It's mostly because our project portfolio has grown tremendously over the last ten years. We have apartment complexes going up all over the city and the suburbs, as well as projects in neighboring cities and even into some parts of Pennsylvania and Ohio.

So yeah, we're growing.

Monica looks up over her glasses when she sees me

come in. "Stephanie, please, take a seat." She motions to one of the chairs in front of the desk. She's all business, donning a still gray suit and her dark hair pulled up out of her face.

I sit and wait for her to finish reading over whatever she's looking at on her computer. Unlike the rest of the office, Monica's office is nearly devoid of any sign of the upcoming holiday. The one lone reminder is the assortment of Christmas cards she has taped on the door of the cabinet above her desk.

The thought of her getting personalized cards from people who care about her actually surprises me. Maybe she's not this stiff at home. Maybe she actually relaxes once in a while.

Finally, Monica turns to me and says, "How are things going?"

I nod, sort of rocking my whole body back and forth, as if to show how enthusiastically I'm trying to be polite. "Everything's okay. Trying to meet several deadlines before the holidays."

"Aren't we all?" Monica offers a quick smile, then goes straight-faced again. For the position she's in and the number of years she's been with the company, she has to be in her late fifties. And if that's the case, she looks good. She's thin, only the slightest hint of wrinkles, although looks are not her focus. She's too practical for that.

"I was wondering how you're doing with the plans for the Kellogg property," she went on. "I need them sooner than later."

Relief washes over me. "Oh! They're all done."

Monica's eyebrows rise. "They are? I didn't see them in our shared folder." She turns back to her computer again and clicks around, as if she would actually call me into her office without first double- and triple-checking that the files weren't there.

"I still need to upload them," I say. "I met with the architects and engineers and they had some change orders they wanted to make, so I spent the last week figuring out those. But everything's all set. I just need to upload the new file."

"Interesting."

My politeness falters a bit. "I'm sorry?"

"Well, I talked to Richard this morning and he says he hasn't seen any updates. He hasn't had a status update in weeks, according to him."

Richard.

That jerk is my so-called "partner" with this specific project, but all he's done is undermine me, belittle me, and get in my way. The truth of the matter is—one that he simply cannot accept—is that I'm a better designer than he is. He thinks Planning and Development is a man's business. He hasn't actually come out and said that, but it's obvious by the way he treats me when we work together.

The trouble is, Monica doesn't like to hear excuses. She only looks at results. And, as it stands, I currently don't have any.

"Well, I—uh—I think Richard may be mistaken," I start. "The plans certainly *are* done. Like I said, I just need to digitize them."

"And yet," Monica says, slowly turning to me from her computer and looking at me over her glasses, "the files have not been uploaded, which is the way we do business around here. You should know that."

"I do. I just didn't think there was any point in uploading an incomplete file—"

"So the plans aren't even done?" Monica cuts in. Her stare is so intense that she intimidates me and I stammer.

"Well—that's not—if you just give me fifteen minutes, I can upload what I have for you to look at."

"And it will have both yours and Richard's signatures on the work?" Monica asks. "I need them both in order to proceed. We don't cut corners around here. Another thing you should know."

"Yes, I'm aware," I say, noticing that I'm suddenly clenching my jaw. "I will find Richard and get his signature before I—"

"Richard took a half day today," Monica interrupts. "He won't be back until next week."

"He did?"

She nods. "Yes. Like I said, I've already talked to him about this project. The trouble is, now these files are late. I have to report to the investors next week and I have no progress on this case to show them.

You see why I have my doubts that they're even finished, don't you?"

"I promise you, they're done. I just need—"

"You know I don't like excuses, Stephanie. If you can't meet our deadlines, then perhaps you need to find employment elsewhere."

My jaw hangs open and my fists clench. There are several choice words on the tip of my tongue, but I hold them in.

Don't burn bridges, my Dad always tells me.

Instead, I rise to my feet. "I think this meeting is over."

Monica has already turned back to her computer. As I leave the room, she mutters, "Yes, you have a lot of work to do to get those files to me by Monday."

DECEMBER 16TH
Steph

She was *completely* dismissive!" I say into the phone back at my apartment. One-handed, I struggle to throw in a load of laundry into the washer and not spill detergent all over the floor.

"Monica can be like that," Lisa says on the other end.

"She wouldn't even *listen* to me! It's like she had her mind made up about the whole situation before she even called me into her office!" I slam the door of the washer closed and hit 'Start.'

Taking a few steps further into the apartment, I collapse on the couch that takes up most of the space. I live in a small one-bedroom. It's a little on the pricy side, but it has nice finishes and a washer and dryer in the unit, so I feel like I'm getting my money's worth.

I let out a heavy sigh. "So I don't know what I'm going to do."

"Did you ever find the plans?" Lisa bangs around on her end too. From the sound of it, she's making dinner.

"Oddly, no," I say. "I was fired up after I left Monica's office, so I searched all over my cubicle for the updated plans, but nada."

"Did you check your apartment? Or maybe your car? Maybe you just misplaced them somewhere."

I shake my head before she's even done talking, not that she can see it over the phone. "No. I *know* I put them in my filing cabinet, but they weren't there."

"How is that possible?"

"My guess is *Richard* has them." I say his name as if it's the most disgusting thing on the planet because, right now, he is to me.

"You don't know that for sure."

"Don't I? He's the one who went to Monica about me. He's the one who *conveniently* took a half day today, when he knew Monica was going to confront me about this. *And* he's not answering my calls! I've tried three times already. All I get is his stupid voicemail where he cheerfully says that he's "taking a few days off."

"Just because he's not answering your calls doesn't mean he stole the plans from you."

"Then maybe Monica has a point," she says.

"Are you *siding* with him? Lisa, he knew I didn't

have a personal phone number for him and now he's avoiding me because he knows I'm upset."

"You just need to relax."

"Don't tell me to relax! I have a right to be angry about this! Richard is trying to take my job!"

"Again, you don't know —"

"What's this sudden fascination with Richard you have? Why do you keep taking his side?"

"I'm not siding with anyone, Steph." She sounds exasperated. "I'm just trying to see things from his side. Look, all I know is that Monica said the plans aren't in the shared folder online where they should be. You claim everything's done and just needs to be signed and uploaded, but you can't find the plans anywhere."

"That's what I *claim* because it's the truth! What do you think I've been working on for the last week?" I ask angrily.

"Of course not," she says. "I'm just saying, maybe you're not as far as you think you are on this project. Maybe you didn't put it in the shared folder because you didn't want Monica or anyone else to see how much you still need to do to it."

"I've written progress reports to go along with the plans. They wouldn't seen what I've been doing. I just don't see the point in scanning and uploading something until it's done, but that's all I have to do."

Lisa sighs. "Okay, so maybe you just need to be more organized."

"I *am* organized!"

"If that were true, Monica never would've called you into her office today."

There's a pause as I process just what Lisa is insinuating. How could she betray me like this? "You know, I called you because I *thought* you'd understand."

"I do, I'm just trying to look at this from all angles instead of jumping right to anger."

"Monica suggested I get another job. How am I not supposed to get angry at that?"

"You're right. But maybe the answer is to take some time off after you find those plans. Relax. Take your mind off work for a bit."

What she says intrigues me. I would love to take time off. And I have it. But with the plans missing, I'm not sure that I can.

"When you come back, maybe you'll remember where you actually put those plans," she adds.

"I put them in the filing cabinet."

She sighs again. "Okay."

"Okay?"

"I'm not going to argue with you about this," she says. Then, quieter, "Apparently that's the only reason you called."

"I called because I needed a friend," I tell her. "Apparently I called the wrong number. But hey, you have a *great* weekend."

And with that, I hang up.

DECEMBER 16TH
Steph

❄ ❄ ❄

My body aches with stress. Every muscle in my body is worn out, as if I've just run a full marathon or, let's be honest, done any kind of exercise at all. I need to calm down.

Stepping to the kitchen, I fix myself a cup of hot chocolate—making sure to drop a peppermint candy in the steam brew for added flavor—and carry it to the couch. Nothing better than to numb the nerves with a bit of rest and relaxation. Watching movies on a Friday night and staying up as late as I feel like sounds like a great way to get my mind off of work and Monica and *Richard*.

Even though it's dinner time, food isn't really on my mind. I'm not hungry. Not for a full meal, at least.

Leaving my hot chocolate on the glass coffee table, I return to the kitchen and make some popcorn in the microwave, greedily dumping the full bag into the largest bowl I have.

Back at the couch, I practice my own version of self-care by burrowing myself into the heap of pillows and blankets with my drink and my snack within reach. Reaching for the remote, I switch to the Hallmark channel for some cheesy, sweet, predicable Christmas movies to ease my soul and calm me down from the day's events. Truly, what I need is to get into the Christmas mood.

The first movie I find is about a woman who comes home for Christmas with a man who is only pretending to be her boyfriend.

Please.

Who comes up with these lame storylines?

Still, the movie soon engrosses me. The male lead is handsome, the supporting characters are quirky and funny, and the main female lead seems to have her head screwed on right, for the most part.

The biggest thing that catches my eye is the small town that seems to be present in nearly every Hallmark Christmas movie. The traditional buildings, the friendly neighbors, the little bell that seems to ring above every storefront door. The snowfall, the decorations, the warmth of family and friends.

I want that kind of Christmas.

The kind of Christmas that Lisa's getting this year. The one she always gets. But after the phone call we just had, there's no way she would even consider an offer to spend the holidays with her in Canandaigua. And really, I'd be using her for something that would feel different for her than it would me. She has connections and history with her family. I would be the tag-along.

No. I don't really want to spend the holidays as the outsider to a tight-knit family tradition. And I don't really want to see Lisa anytime soon. Not until I hear an apology.

Maybe I'll feel differently about that in the morning, but I still can't crash her Christmas.

Thoughts of a traditional small town Christmas distract me from the movie and I find myself reaching for my phone. I need something to cheer me up. To distract me from my life. Something bigger than a movie and a night in. I'm bound and determined to have a happy Christmas this year. It's too easy to have a lonely, depressing one when you're spending the day by yourself. If I have to be by myself, I should do it in style.

Pulling up the Airbnb app, I search for cute rentals in my price range in Canandaigua. Being a lakefront city a week before Christmas, most rentals are booked up. And I don't really want to be in the same small town as Lisa. If it's anything like Hallmark, I'm bound to run into her, who will probably bring up work and I want to forget about that.

I switch over to Google Maps and zoom out of Rochester, searching for another nearby small town. My eye immediately lands on Batavia. After a few more taps, I determine it's only about a half hour drive from my apartment. Far enough to be different, close enough that I don't need to spend a lot of time traveling.

Back on the Airbnb app, I search for rentals and find a whole house that's in my price range and immaculately decorated for Christmas. Cozy fireplace, large kitchen, a master suite with a full-size tub.

Sold!

I check the dates. It's available as early as tomorrow.

Something in the back of my head makes me wonder what the catch is, but I don't want to delay on this sweet deal. I follow the prompts all the way to the last one that tells me to "Book Now."

I consider it further. I *do* have the days. I could take a full week off, have an extended vacation, and return to the office the week between Christmas and New Year's to soak up what's left of my job before Monica inevitably lets me go. But would that be professional? Shouldn't I stay and submit those plans before I take a vacation?

"What the hell?" I murmur to myself. The plans

are already late. Monica's already planning to meet with investors and having to schmooze them until I can come up with something. And the week after Christmas will be quiet in the office. Even if those plans never show up, I should be able to make the changes over again and still have them turned in by the New Year.

On my phone, I hit "Book Now." Minutes later, I'm pulling up email and telling Monica that I'm taking the next week off.

DECEMBER 16TH
Carson

＊ ＊ ＊

When the Nicholsons pull up the driveway, I breathe a sigh of relief. I've been watching for them from the living room window. It's always better when clients are on time. No matter how many times I've done this, standing in a stranger's house before the clients gets to the house is always awkward. Like I'm intruding in someone's personal space, because, well, I am.

As Carol and Nigel make their way up the sidewalk, I greet them at the front door, swinging it open into the cold mid-December air.

"Hi! So glad you found it okay!" My realtor smile is plastered on my face. It's a mix between genuine affection and just wanting to close a deal.

"Almost missed the turn down the street," Carol says with a smile. She has a tight grip on the handrail to climb the two steps up to the concrete porch.

"These cul-de-sacs are confusing," Nigel adds. "And then add the snow? Forget it." He waits for his wife to climb the steps before he does.

"I grew up on the east side of Buffalo and all the street were a grid," Carol says. "Navigating them was easy, pronouncing all those Polish street names was the hard part!"

I laugh. "Well, I don't think you'll have any trouble with Oakwood Drive." This whole neighborhood is made up of small brick ranches in a mix of twisted, cul-de-sac streets named after generic tree-like things that were probably made up in a developer's mind back in the sixties. Even though I'm not a fan of the brick ranches, they're what sells. And if I don't sell, I don't get paid.

"Looks like the whole neighborhood is kept up nice," Nigel says as they step inside. "Everyone's driveway seems to be cleared of the snow. Most houses even had Christmas decorations out. Really brightens up the street."

"Most of the houses in this area are similar to this one," I say. "Two bedrooms, one bathroom, open floor plan, good-sized yard."

"This is very nice," Carol says, looking around the great room. "Could use some personal touches, but even without those you can tell this is a good house."

"Dear, we haven't seen any of it yet," Nigel tells her.

After they've taken off their snowy shoes and left them near the door, I show them around the large room. It's not like there's much to show, being one giant room, but I still make an effort to point out the granite countertops, the laminate flooring, and the separate dining, living, and kitchen areas.

"We could easily host the holidays here," Carol tells Nigel. "Everyone would be together."

"Yes, that would be nice," he murmurs, glancing outside. "The property goes to that fence there?"

I nod. "That's right. And there's a shed in the corner too, so you can hold all of your yard tools. And there's plenty of room for a garden."

Carol shakes her head. "I can't be in the sun too long, so I'm not much of a gardener, but Nigel usually keeps the yard looking nice."

"No trees," he murmurs. "Can't imagine what the heating and cooling bills will be."

"There's plenty of room to plant a tree if you'd like."

"And have to pick up sticks every spring and fall? Forget it."

I manage to keep a friendly smile, even though his comment irks me. When I became a realtor, these were not the houses I expected to sell. The boxy, unimaginative duplicates coated in various shades of grays and whites with no trees, sidewalks, or any hint of character at all.

"Down the hall are the bedrooms," I say. "First door on the left is the bathroom, if you want to take a look at that."

"The only bathroom?" Nigel grunts.

"Yes."

"So no master?" Carol asks.

I shake my head. "Not with an en suite. But the largest bedroom is right on the other side of the wall. You could easily put in another door and create a sort of Jack and Jill bathroom."

"We're too old to get involved with any kind of renovation," Nigel dismisses.

"You could hire it out," I suggest. "Or I could show you houses with en suites. I wasn't sure that's what you were looking for. With those, there's two bathrooms and brings up the cost of the house, and that's obviously something to consider. But I could take a look."

"These rooms are a decent size." Carol looks steps inside and looks around. The chain from the ceiling fan hangs low, brushing against the top of her hair, but she doesn't seem to notice.

Nigel opens the closet and grumbles when he sees what it holds. They're pretty big, considering the square footage of the house. The grunt must've been because he couldn't find anything to complain about.

"The utility room is at the end of the hall," I tell them, leading them back into the narrow hallway. "You have your hot water tank and washer and dryer hook-ups right there."

"Is there a basement?" Nigel asks.

I shake my head. "Only a crawl space."

"So where is the electrical panel?"

"In the back of the closet pantry near the kitchen," I say. "It's easily accessible if you ever need to get at it."

Nigel harrumphs as we all shuffle back to the main living space.

"Please, feel free to take a look at anything else you want to further inspect," I tell them.

Carol looks to her husband. "I think we've seen enough. What do you think, honey?"

"Yeah, I'm ready to go. I don't think this is the house for us."

"Okay, well, I can look around and—"

"Carson, I don't mean to be rude, but you've shown us nearly ten houses already and we haven't liked a single one," Nigel says.

Because you keep changing what you're looking for that I can't find the imaginary house that only exists in your mind, I think to myself. I've had nearly enough of this couple, but right now they're my only clients. I need to be nice to them to make another sale before Christmas, which would prevent my boss from letting me go from the agency.

"We know you're working hard," Carol says. "We just think that maybe we'd have luck with another agent."

"Oh," I say, still trying to be as non-confrontational as possible. "Okay. Well, if you change your mind, you still have my card."

"Yes, we do." Nigel turns to his wife. "Come on, honey. We need to be getting home before this storm rolls in."

Carol gives me one last mournful look before she steps through the front door.

December 16th
Carson

❄ ❄ ❄

The keys hit the table by the door with a clang, ringing out into the empty house. The Christmas lights haven't kicked on just yet, so inside the house is dark, even if outside is still decently bright from the setting sun.

As I make my way back to my bedroom, the Christmas lights click on with the help of the timers. Grandpa always tried to get them as in-sync as possible. He would fuss with them right up until Christmas Day, trying to get everything to come on at once.

Man, I miss him.

After I change out of the suit I wore to show the Nicholsons the house they used to fire me, I reheat the food in the Tupperware in the fridge. Someone suggested that I try meal prepping to save time and stay on track with my diet, not that I care that much about the latter. While it's nice to not have to cook every night, it's boring to eat the same thing every night.

Still, I take the Tupperware into the living room, which is now sufficiently lit by the Christmas lights alone, and plop on the couch. Leaning over the coffee table, I grab the remote control and turn on the TV.

Last year I wanted to cancel cable in favor of on-demand options, but Grandpa insisted we keep it because he wanted to watch the news and the Thanksgiving Day parade and other live events. Ever since he passed, I still haven't brought myself to cancel it.

While I wait for my food to cool enough to eat, I flip through the channels. Memories come flooding back to me of sitting on the couch while Grandpa channel-surfed, much to my displeasure and shouts for him to stop at something that looked good.

I thought that days without him would get easier, but the truth is I've only adjusted to his absence out of necessity. I still wish he were here. And this being the first Christmas season without him doesn't make things any easier. He wasn't just family, he was my best friend. Someone I could talk to about anything. He would've listened to me about my bad day today. He would've encouraged me that things were going to work out. That something special was right around the corner.

Grandpa has been there for me for nearly as long as I can remember. From the little he told me, my father never stuck around when he found out my mother was pregnant with me. And my mother eventually fell in with the wrong crowd, continuing to leave me with Grandpa so she could go out and party.

When I was ten years old, she got in a bad car accident on her way back from a bar. Grandpa getting custody of me was the obvious choice. He had basically been my only parent my whole life anyway. Everything I am and everything I have achieved is because of him.

On the TV, I search for something cheerful that will get my mind off of my grandfather's absence.

I land on this one movie about a woman trying to get home for the holidays. It's terribly cheesy and stereotypical, but it holds my interest for a bit while I eat. If nothing else, the Christmas decorations in the set look amazing. Certainly better than that drab ranch I showed today.

Throughout the movie, flashback scenes to the woman's childhood show up. Caroling in the snow, going to get a Christmas tree, ice skating, wrapping presents, making cookies. All the usuals for the holidays.

The movie is predictable, absolutely, but I find myself feeling sad and nostalgic for the way things used to be when I was younger. Grandpa would always sing Christmas songs terribly in the car, just to embarrass me. He wasn't usually one for singing, but when the radio started playing the Christmas songs, something changed in him.

And every year we would go get our Christmas tree from a farm out in Genesee County. I remember the first time he let me help him cut it and how much work I thought it was. I was probably around six at that point.

The one year he made me an ice rink in the backyard with the house. It was a mess when spring came around, but boy did I get my use out of that makeshift ice rink.

Shoot. I better not start crying. What the heck is wrong with me? Grief is a weird thing, that's for sure. I force myself to stop recalling the memories and simply watch the movie, but it's hard not to let my mind wander.

Even after I finish my dinner, I sit back and continue watching the movie. It's not so bad once you get over the terrible acting. To be honest, the plot has me hooked to see how it's going to play out, even though it's very obvious how it's going to play out.

One of the major downside of cable: commercials. When one comes on, I instinctively reach for my phone. But instead of opening up the usual social media apps, I find myself opening up Airbnb.

I've tried to dress up this house as best I could on my own. Tried to celebrate the season so I didn't automatically go into a depression every time I came home. But no matter how many lights and tchotchkes I put out, Grandpa will still be missing from the Christmas season this year. I can't reverse that. I need an escape.

Having Christmas in a different house in a different town is just what I need. It's not like I'll be missing out on spending it with friends and family. All my friends have plans and Grandpa was the last of my family. If I'm going to be alone, then it should at least be a deliberate decision and not an unfortunate circumstance.

I find a nice-looking Airbnb in Batavia, which is roughly thirty miles away from my suburban Buffalo house. And, not too farm from where Grandpa used to take me to get our Christmas tree every year.

Perfect.

I hit "Book," type in my credit card information, and complete the transaction before the movie comes back on.

DECEMBER 17TH

Steph

* * *

As soon as I pull into the driveway, the owner pulls in right behind me. Taylor, according to her Airbnb profile. She has bright blonde hair, a white puffy coat with faux fur lining the hood, and black leather boots that come up to her knees. She gets out and greets me at the front door of the house, holding up a pair of keys on a keyring.

"I'm so glad you found it!" she says with a bright smile. "Did you have any trouble?"

"Nope. I just plugged it into my GPS on my phone." I shake her gloved hand. "It wasn't that hard."

"Oh good. Yeah, it's right on a main route, which makes getting here pretty easy, even if it means a little more traffic. I'm Taylor, by the way."

"Stephanie," I say. "But everyone calls me Steph."

"How cute!" She turns to unlock the door.

I look down the busy street and try to spot any signs of the cute shops I saw in the pictures online. Hopefully this isn't one of those rentals where it turns out too good to be true.

"Where is everything?"

Taylor looks at me, a slight furrow in her brow. "What do you mean?"

"It's just, from the pictures it looked like the house was right in the center of everything," I say. "This road is certainly busy, but…"

"Oh, Main Street is not that far away," Taylor assures me. "The whole city stretches along the length of it, so just down the street from here is Main, and then it's just a quick right and you're straight in the action."

I nod and look down the street. It's hard to tell exactly what kind of walking conditions it is with all the snowfall. It's been picking up since I left my apartment. Nothing too hazardous, but certainly a sign that it's winter.

Taylor opens the door and we step into the warm house. She kicks off the snow from her boots, then slides them off and steps into the spacious living room.

There's hardwood floors all over. A staircase tucked along one wall with a hallway behind it leading to the first floor bathroom and bedroom. To the back of the living room—which has obviously been expanded in a remodel that sacrificed some walls—is the entry to the kitchen.

"Here we are!" Taylor beams. "I've decorated the place a bit, so I hope you feel right at home."

There's garland down the staircase banister, a tiny fake pine tree in the corner near the fireplace, and a red and black plaid blanket draped over the large black leather sectional situated in front of a large-screen TV.

"It looks great," I say.

Taylor steps to the kitchen and points out the stocked pantry, the coffee counter, and the condiments in the fridge. "I only keep non-perishable foods here, but help yourself to whatever you want!"

"Thank you."

The kitchen is large, with an angled island, cabinets to the ceiling, and plenty of room for the dining table on the other side of the room. There are lots of windows, which look nice, but I can already feel a draft on my toes, even with my fuzzy socks. I probably won't be spending a lot of time in here if I can help it.

Taylor walks me back out to the living room and stands at the hall behind the stairs. "The master is down here, with its own en suite bathroom. Then the guest half-bath is right next to the door for the master, so you have options. There should be plenty of towels and blankets down here already, but if you need more there's a linen closet at the top of the stairs." She pauses and looks around. "Um…what else? Oh! I have all kinds of shampoos and conditioners and body wash, but if you run out, check the closet in the upstairs hallway. Again, help yourself to whatever you need during your stay."

I nod again. "Thank you. I really appreciate everything."

"What are you planning on doing here while you're in town?"

"Mostly have a relaxing holiday alone," I say.

"You have to check out Main Street downtown. There's all kinds of restaurants and a few shops. We're small, but our downtown is getting more interesting every year. Actually, there's a new bakery and bookstore that just opened on Jackson Street. It's called Books and Bakes. The couple that owns it is so great!"

"Can I walk there?"

Taylor hesitates. "Well…you *could*. It's a bit of a walk in nice weather. I wouldn't recommend it in this weather, but there's *plenty* of parking downtown!"

I shrug. "I think I'll be able to brave it. I'm originally from Maine, so the cold doesn't really bother me."

"Well, then, in that case, this should be a piece of cake!" She steps over toward the couch and points out the papers spread on the coffee table. "I have the

WiFi password listed, as well as my phone number and directions to any emergency services. Hopefully you won't need any of those! But feel free to call or text me if you need anything. Okay?"

Another nod. "Sounds good, thank you!"

"Enjoy!"

After she leaves, I take a lap around the house to inspect everything closer. The three bedrooms upstairs are smaller than the one downstairs and there is only one bathroom for that whole floor. Meanwhile, the master has the largest bed, a spacious bathroom, and a clawfoot bathtub that I see myself taking a dip in by the end of the day.

Back at the door, I lace up my boots, and bundle up for the weather. Before I set off downtown, I check to make sure I have my wallet with me. I debate whether I want to bring in my bags from the car now, but decide on doing it later when I get back.

On my way out, I lock the door and start down what my GPS called Clinton Street on the way here. If Taylor's directions are correct, all I need to do is take Clinton to Main and turn right and then I'll be downtown.

Piece of cake.

As I get further down Clinton, I wonder how many people walk in this town. At least on this street. The trek to Main isn't terrible, but it isn't great. It isn't until I reach East Avenue that I realize I had been walking on the shoulder of the road since I left the house. I had just assumed the sidewalks were buried under the snow, but it turns out there weren't any until East Avenue.

Even after I am correctly on the sidewalk, it seems only every other house has them cleared. I know from work that Rochester expects homeowners to clear the sidewalks in front of their house. If the homeowner doesn't, the city does it and then fines them for the work.

Apparently, that's not the same here in Batavia.

It seems through the whole duration of my walk, the wind is at my face. I might be from Maine, but cold is cold. And the wind chill still makes it colder.

When I finally make it downtown, I try to take in my options and look around before I dart in the first building I see. But I only make it one street over before I give up and go into the first restaurant I can.

It's a local brewery and I sidle up to the bar, shivering in my jacket as the warmth of the restaurant surrounds me.

"What can I get for you?" the bartender asks. She has long tresses and is wearing a T-shirt sporting the name of the brewery right across her chest.

Glancing up at the drink menu on the chalkboard above the bar, I make a quick selection. "Um…number two. Is that any good?"

"One of my favorites." She reaches below the counter and pulls out a clean glass, taking a few steps over to fill it from the tap.

When she passes it back to me, I hand her my card.

She studies it, then looks at me. "Are you new in town? I've never seen a card from this bank before."

"Yeah, it's a local bank from out in Maine," I tell her. "I never really got around to switching banks when I moved to Rochester."

As she runs my card, she asks, "What brought you all the way out here from Maine?"

"Work," I say plainly. "Not a lot of architecture firms out my way."

"That's cool. You want me to keep your tab open, sweetie?"

"Um, do you have a lunch menu? I'm starving."

"Oh sure." She goes to the other end of the bar, retrieves a menu, and brings it back to me. "Everything here is delicious and locally sourced."

"How neat!" I say with a grin as I open the menu and start to take a look.

The bartender takes an order for someone down the bar and then comes back to take my order. "I'll put that right in for you."

When she's gone, I sip my beer—delicious—and look around. The place has a very cool vibe. A little industrial, with nods to its history as well as the community.

"So if you live in Rochester," the bartender starts, "what brings you to Batavia today? Meeting a friend?"

"I'm on vacation, actually."

She looks confused. "Here?"

I laugh. "Yeah. I wanted a small town."

"Well, you certainly got it."

"I'm Steph, by the way," I say.

She smiles. "Cameron. So, what are you going to do while you're here?"

I shrug. "Not really sure. Probably just relax. Do you have any suggestions?"

"If you're looking for action, you came to the wrong place," she says with a chuckle. "It's an aging community, so most people hunker down for the holidays. There are some things to do, but unless you know someone in a community band or something, you probably wouldn't be interested."

I make a face. Even though I want that small town feel, I don't want to get the strange looks from people who don't recognize me from around town. I'm sure nobody would say anything, but still.

"But who knows?" Cameron says. "Some people around here would love to see new faces in the community."

True. If nothing else, I could *try* to meet new people. After all, I am on this trip alone. Wouldn't want to be alone on Christmas.

"I'm going to go check on your food," she tells me. "I'll be right back."

The meal Cameron brings out is delicious, just as she said it would be. As I eat, I notice how the snowfall has only gotten heavier since I arrived. So I don't spend anymore time chitchatting with Cameron and I head out. Maybe I can come back here later on my trip and talk to her some more. She seems very nice.

As I bundle up to brave the cold again, I debate whether I should just take an Uber back, but my pride gets the better of me. Besides, how many Ubers are really available out here? I'd be better off hitching a ride from someone and I've watched too many murder mysteries to fall for that mistake.

Looks like I'm walking it again.

It's another forty-five minutes before I make it back to the house. I nearly missed it because of how much it's snowed since then. My car is barely visible in the driveway, but I unbury the back side door to retrieve my bags.

With numb fingers, I struggle to get the bags inside, but I manage. My body tingles as the warmth hits me.

Being the Maine native that I am, I know I need to get my body warm after being in the cold for so long. And I've been thinking about that bathtub the whole way back.

Peeling off my coat and boots, I set them by the door and drag my suitcases into the master bedroom. I slide the suitcases into the closet and then immediately peel off my wet clothes. Naked and shivering, I run the bath and pull out a towel from the decorative shelf in the corner.

With the tub filled, I dip my toes in and feel the wonderful sting on my skin from the hot water. Slowly, I submerge my whole body and rest my head back. After that walk in the cold, this feels amazing.

I'm not sure how long I sit there. Perhaps I even fell asleep, but when I finally open my eyes, I jump.

There's a man standing in the doorway of the bathroom.

We both jump. Me splashing in the tub and the man stepping back into the bedroom.

"What the hell is wrong with you!" I shout. "Who are you!" The worst possible scenarios run through my head.

"Sorry!" he says, covering his eyes. "I didn't think anyone would be here!"

I stand up and reach for my towel, but slip in my rush and splash back into the tub.

"Do you need help?" he asks, looking back into the room.

"Don't look!" I shout. Any trace of cold is gone as my body flushes with embarrassment.

By time I've wrapped a towel around my wet body, Taylor has joined the party.

"I'm so sorry!" she says. "Uh, Carson, why don't we go wait in the living room and I can explain everything once Steph is decent?"

They leave me alone, closing the bedroom door as they go, not that it matters anymore. I tighten the towel around my chest, then reach for the robe hanging on the back of the door and throw that on as well. With my wet hair dangling down my back, I step into the living room and fold my arms, trying not to think about how a complete stranger has just seen me naked.

"I'm so sorry," Taylor says again when she sees me.

"What happened? Why are you here? And who is this?"

"This is Carson," Taylor says. "He's…also my guest."

"Where?" I ask.

"Here."

"Here?"

She nods. "The app must've malfunctioned somehow and—"

"What are you trying to say?" I shuffle my feet, trying not to draw attention to the puddle pooling around my feet.

"I accidentally double-booked." Taylor cringes. "I'm so sorry!"

"So we've both technically booked the house for the next week?" Carson asks her.

She nods. "Unfortunately."

"I'm not leaving," I say defiantly. "I got here first."

"And I can totally understand that," Taylor says.

"Well, hold on," he says. "That's not exactly fair."

"You just walked in on me in the tub!" I snap. "*Fair* is out the window."

"Hold on. There's a solution here," Taylor says as a moderator. "I'd be willing to offer a refund and even provide a discount for the next stay because of all of this."

I don't dare look in Carson's eyes, even though he's trying to catch mine.

"When did you book it?" he asks me.

"Last night."

"So did I."

"What time?"

"I don't know? Seven?"

"I booked it at five-thirty," he says.

Taylor nods and looks at her phone. "That's what my emails state too."

I eye up both of them, annoyed that this man—*Carson*—is actually entitled to be here and not me.

Carson looks out the window at the heavy falling snow. Then he looks back at me and somehow I feel more exposed than when I was flopping around naked in the tub.

Okay, maybe that was worse than this.

He sighs. "I'm not going to make you go out in this weather when you've *obviously* gotten comfortable. You can stay."

"So you're leaving?" I ask.

"I didn't say that."

"So what *are* you saying?"

The two of us exchange looks and then turn to Taylor, who shrugs.

"The house is plenty big enough for two people," she says quietly. "That is, if you both don't mind."

"You want us to stay here *together*?" I ask.

"It sounds like Carson's okay with it."

"I'm willing to try," he says.

"This is ridiculous!"

"There are separate bathrooms, bedrooms, and a finished lounge space in the attic that Carson can claim since you have the living room," Taylor says. "The only thing the two of you would have to share is the kitchen."

Carson looks to me and grins. "Sounds like a good compromise to me."

I wanted to be alone this week, but I also thought I had rented a house closer to town. It doesn't look like I'm going back into town anytime soon, unless I unbury my car. So maybe having some company wouldn't be so bad after all.

"Fine," I finally say. "We can give it a shot."

December 17th
Carson

❄ ❄ ❄

"Do you need a hand?"

I look up from my work shoveling the driveway and see a man walking up from the street. He's bundled up in coveralls, heavy boots, and a heavy jacket. He pulls off his gloves as he approaches and I can see the faint drip of sweat on his brow, just below his hat line.

How anyone could be sweating in this cold is beyond me. And I'm even moving pretty good with all this physical labor.

"You need a hand?" he repeats as he gets closer. "I've got my snowblower out still. Two or three swipes is all it would take to finish this off for you."

I size up what I have left—I still need to unbury both

cars—and then turn back to him. "Uh, sure. If you don't mind."

"Not at all." He starts to turn away, then looks back at me. He extends his hand. "I'm Paul. I live across the street with my wife. We keep an eye on the place for Taylor and help out with some of the outside upkeep."

Pulling off my glove, I shake his hand. "Carson. I just got here today."

"Did your wife get here before you?" he asks.

Observant, I think.

"She's not my wife," I clarify. "Taylor accidentally overbooked the place so we're both staying here. The other guest's name is Steph. She's not too happy about the situation, so I thought I'd come out here and give her some space."

Paul laughs. "And doing her a favor by unburying her car. Smart man. How long are you in town for?"

"Just until after Christmas," I say. "I'm not sure about Steph, though. I'm not that familiar with the area. Is there anything I should check out while I'm here?"

"Well, there are some nice trails down at the county park," he says. "My wife and I go cross-country skiing down there sometimes. It's about a fifteen or twenty minute drive, though. As far as things in town, there are some great restaurants downtown on Main Street. I would definitely give those a try. And a few shops that you could look around at."

I nod. "I'll check those out. Thanks."

"Well, let me get my snowblower so I can get this stuff finished up for you before we need to start again."

"Thanks."

"While I'm running back across the street, why don't you try to clean off the cars as much as possible? I may as well blow that snow away along with everything else."

"Will do."

When he turns to leave, I immediately put my gloves back on, hoping to get some feeling in my fingers back. But the inside of my gloves are wet from my sweat, so my gloves are equally cold. The former Boy Scout in me reminds me that I need to hurry up and get inside before frost bite sets in.

By time Paul comes back, I've cleared off most of the snow off of our cars. The roar of the engine on his snowblower prevents any talk longer than a "thank you" and a "let me know if you need anything else."

As Paul sets off back to his house with the driveway mostly cleared, I retreat back into the house to get out of the cold. As soon as the door is behind me and the warmth envelopes me, I feel immediate relief.

Steph has commandeered the living room. She's wrapped in a blanket on the sectional. *Home Alone* plays on the big screen TV. An empty bowl sits beside her, which presumably once held popcorn.

"The driveway is clear," I announce as I peel off my jacket and kick off my boots.

She doesn't say anything and I wonder if she's asleep, but I see her reach for her phone so I know that's not the case. She's ignoring me.

Okay then. Still mad.

"I'm a little sweaty, so I'm going up to take a shower," I say. A smirk comes across my face and I add, "Just letting you know, in case you want to walk in on me to even the score."

Finally, she looks at me and offers a glare.

I grin and hold her stare.

Reluctantly, a smile starts to creep on her face and she turns back to her phone, feigning disinterest.

"Was that a smile?" I tease.

Steph turns back to the TV.

In my socks, I step to the back of the couch so I know she can hear me. "Look, I really am sorry for scaring you earlier. And for the whole mix-up. I know it wasn't really my fault, but I also know this isn't exactly the kind of vacation you probably envisioned."

She chews on the inside of her cheek. Her eyes are laser-focused on the movie.

Message received. She doesn't want to talk.

Turning, I head upstairs and scope out my room and the second floor bathroom, which I guess is all mine during my stay.

It's small—certainly original—but it'll do. My bedroom is a little tight, fitting just a queen-sized bed, a night stand, and a dresser wedged into the corner, but the bed seems comfortable enough. Most importantly, the pillows are the right firmness. Most hotels have pillows that are too fluffy. Others seem to put rocks in pillowcases and call it a day. This is a nice happy-medium. My Goldilocks pillows, if you will.

After I shower and change into sweatpants, I come downstairs to fix something to eat. The sun has already started to wane and my stomach is gurgling from the exercise of shoveling the large driveway.

To my surprise, Steph is in the kitchen, even as *Home Alone 2: Lost in New York* plays in the living room. The kitchen is much colder than the living room and I make a mental note to pull out my wool socks from upstairs.

"Oh. Hi." It's all I can think of to say when I enter the kitchen.

She has two plates in front of her, each with a single sandwich on it. She slides one my way. "Here. I made you a peanut butter and jelly."

I frown and take a seat on the bar stool on the opposite side of the island. "Thanks."

"What? Don't tell me you don't like PB & J. If that's the case, we're really getting off on the wrong foot here."

I'm glad she's actually trying, but still I feel a pang of sadness. Grandpa used to religiously have PB & J every day for lunch. And whenever both of us happened to be home for lunch, that's what he'd make me one too.

"No, I love it," I tell her.

"Well, someone needs to tell your face."

I smirk. "Sorry. It's just an old memory. Funny how those things spring up on you at the most random times, right?"

"I guess I've never had any kind of emotional reaction to a sandwich before."

"It's nothing," I say quickly. "Thanks for making it. I appreciate it."

"Well, thanks for shoveling, even if it was probably a waste. And even though you did get help from the neighbor."

I shrug as I bring the sandwich up to take a bite. "Got me out of the house, which I think we both needed. How long are you staying?"

Steph tugs off the crust. "The plan was to stay through until Christmas."

I gulp down my bite as I nod. "That's what I'm doing too."

"But now I'm not so sure that that's the case."

"What do you mean?"

She waves between us. "This is awkward, isn't it?"

"What do you mean?" I hold up my half-eaten

sandwich. "We're breaking bread together. We're already warming up!" I grin again as I take another bite. After I swallow, I add, "Seriously, there's no reason two strangers can't celebrate Christmas together. Isn't that what the spirit of the season is all about? Enjoying everyone's company?"

Steph raises her eyebrows and nods. She's successfully peeled off the crust around the top layer of bread. "I guess so. It's just…weird. I mean, we don't know each other."

"So let's get to know each other. I'm all for extra company if you are."

"I don't make friends easily."

"It's a good thing no one else is here to distract us." I pop the last of my sandwich in my mouth.

"How do I know you're not a serial killer?"

"*Me?*" I ask. "You're the one tearing her sandwich apart with no remorse!"

She catches herself and grins. Then she picks it up and takes a bite. "Happy?"

"Very. Put that poor thing out of its misery."

Another grin. Guess I'm doing something right.

"I promise you I'm not a serial killer," I say. "Just for the record. And I'm not some other kind of weirdo, either."

"What's another kind of weirdo?"

"The Peeping Tom kind."

She makes a face. "Well, I wasn't worried about *that* until just now."

"Hey, if it makes you feel any better, you can lock your bedroom door every night."

Steph looks up at me and hooks an eyebrow with a grin. "Serial killers kill in the daytime too."

"Do they? Seems like something a serial killer would know. Maybe *I* should be the one afraid of *you*."

She rolls her eyes. "It's not so much you as much as the fact that I was looking forward to staying in alone."

"We can be alone together."

"That's not what I meant. This is awkward. How are we supposed to spend the holidays together?"

"We get to know each other," I say. "But you're right. I think this is a bit awkward."

"See," she says with a flourish in my direction. "Even you admit it."

"Yeah. This house is doing *okay* in the decorations department, but it could really use some more. Like, I don't know, maybe a *Christmas tree*! What do you say? You and my go out tomorrow and get one? We can get some cheap ornaments and lights, string some popcorn and make it really nice."

"And you think that'll make it less awkward?"

"Couldn't hurt," I say with a shrug. "Think of it as a bonding experience. Like college orientation with your new roommate."

"I hated college."

"So did I," I admit. "At least, that first week.

Anyway, if nothing else, getting a Christmas tree together will help make this place not look so depressing at night."

She smiles. "Fine. We'll go tomorrow and get a tree."

December 18th

Steph

* * *

"This one's cute." I point out a tree that's about as tall as me.

"Bigger," Carson says and keeps walking.

We're walking through the selection of Christmas trees at Harrington's, which is this farmer's market-type store that sells homemade goods year-round. Unfortunately, the trees have been severely picked over. Who buys a Christmas tree less than a week before Christmas? That's the kind of desperate thing you see in movies to add aesthetic, but never did I think I'd be doing it in real life.

Of course, never did I think I'd be spending Christmas without a Christmas tree. Or with a total stranger.

"How much do you expect to shell out for this thing?" I wrap my hands around my coffee to warm them.

Harrington's is the third place we've been to look for a Christmas tree. Everyone else is sold out. On the way through town, Carson stopped at the local coffee shop downtown and got us both coffees. The barista threw in a dash of peppermint in mine, which helps give it that holiday cheer I didn't realize I needed in my life.

"I don't know," he says. "I just know we need a good tree."

"And what about lights?"

"I texted Taylor this morning. She said there's some in the garage."

"You already talked to her about it?" *Well, hasn't he thought of everything today?* I think to myself.

Our feet crunch in the snow as we move around the selection of leftover trees. Mostly Charlie Brown trees, but there are some decent ones here too.

I adjust my mittens to make sure there's no possibility of a draft. Harrington's is just down the street from our rental, but the gentle breeze blowing off the roof is enough to send chills right to the bone.

"I wanted to make sure she had the water basin and everything too," he says. "Some people are weird about what we can bring into their houses."

"True." I take a sip. "It *is* her house, after all."

"Here." He stops in front of one that's about a foot taller than him. "What do you think?"

"It's pretty, but it's—" I step forward and pull at the tag. "—about a hundred dollars more than I was thinking. So that's a no."

Carson shrugs. "I'll pay the extra."

I raise my eyebrows, which lifts my knitted hat with the pompom on top. "Are you sure? That's a lot of money for something we're only going to have a week."

"You'll be thankful for it when it's lighting up the room."

"If you say so."

We go inside and pay, then I sit in the car and finish my coffee while Carson struggles to get it up on the roof. He has ropes and ties and tries to get the tree secured to the roof racks, but he has a hard time reaching.

At one point, he's nearly pressed against the window, jacket and shirt raising to reveal his stomach as he stretches to reach the cord.

"Do you need help?" I ask when he's back on the ground and fixing his clothing.

"No, I can get it," he says with an edge of frustration.

"If you say so." I take another sip of my coffee.

After a few more minutes, another car pulls up and a couple gets out. As they head around to the Christmas tree lot, the man turns to Carson and asks him something that I can't quite make out from inside the car.

Before I can decipher what he said, both men are on either side of the car, fastening the straps to the roof racks. Meanwhile, the woman stands under the covered porch of the store, watching and waiting.

When the men finish, they both retreat back to the woman and begin chatting. Carson shakes her hand. Formal introductions are being made and I figure I should get out and be polite.

"Hi," I say as I walk up to them. I bury my hands in my pockets. My coffee is mostly gone so it wouldn't have helped keep me warm. I left it in the car.

"This is Adam and Tanya," Carson tells me.

I shake both of their hands. "I'm Steph."

"Nice to meet you," Tanya says.

"Carson says you guys are here for the holidays," Adam says. "How long are you guys in town for?"

"Just until after Christmas," I say.

"We're staying at the Airbnb up here on Clinton." Carson points in the direction. "Do you know it?"

Adam laughs. "Oh yeah. I know it."

"Taylor is his ex-wife," Tanya clarifies.

My eyes grow wide. "Oh." Things just turned awkward.

"It's okay." Adam is still humored by our surprise. "We're on decent terms now. We've both moved on. Actually, I helped her fix up the place when she bought it last year. I'm a contractor."

Carson nods. "Oh cool. I'm a real estate agent."

"What agency?"

"Rhodes and Company," Carson says. "We're fairly small, based mostly in Cheektowaga, although I've sold houses in Lancaster and Depew as well."

Things that I didn't even know about him. Not that I should be surprised. We just met twenty-four hours ago.

"Do you work in real estate too?" Tanya asks me.

"Oh. No. I work for an architecture firm out in Rochester."

Adam looks between us, confused. "Do you guys live in Albion or Warsaw or something? They're kind of in the middle between Buffalo and Rochester."

I shake my head. "No, I live in Rochester and he lives…" I trail off, not sure where exactly Carson lives.

"In Cheektowaga," he says, then adds, "We're not together."

"Oh," Tanya says. "But aren't you staying at Taylor's place together?"

"Yeah," Carson says.

"It's a long story," I say. "Anyway, thanks for helping Carson with the tree. It was nice talking to you."

"Do you need any help getting it down and in the house?" Adam asks. "It's right down the street, so not out of the way at all."

"No thanks," Carson says. "We'll manage."

"All right then. Take it easy."

"Merry Christmas!" Tanya calls as they turn toward the tree lot.

Back in the car, I shiver and damn myself for not turning it on while Carson loaded up to warm up the car.

"So there's someone else who thought we were a couple," Carson says as he maneuvers out of the parking lot.

"Who else thought that?"

"The neighbor across the street from the house."

"You set him straight, right?"

"Yeah. But it's kind of fun to get that same expression on people's faces."

I roll my eyes. "That's mean."

"It's all innocent," he says. "Besides I set them straight."

"Sure. Oh, let me give you my share for the tree." I dig in my purse for cash, but Carson waves his hand at me.

"Don't worry about it."

"But it was expensive."

"So? I told you, it's my treat."

"But it's for something we're only going to have a couple days."

"And it was my suggestion to begin with."

I let out a frustrated sigh. "Are you trying to be difficult?"

"No. I'm trying to be generous. It's the season of giving, after all."

I roll my eyes, then look over at him. We're just turning into the driveway now. "So you're not going to take the money?"

"Nope." He shifts into park and turns off the car.

Slightly annoyed at his refusing to take my money, I simply stand back and watch as he unties the ropes that he and Adam worked so hard at fastening.

"Do you want me to set up the water basin?" I ask.

"Already did it before we left."

"You did?" I look toward the house as he runs up to unlock the door.

"You were busy primping in the bathroom, so you probably didn't even notice."

"I'm on vacation, I can take as long as I want," I shoot back.

He props the door open and offers me a smile. "Quit belly-aching and help me get this inside before we lose all the heat from the house and rack up Taylor's fuel bill."

I take hold of the trunk of the tree while he takes the top. We get it inside, pine needles and snow falling all over the hardwood. I nearly step into the water basin as I back up toward the corner where Carson put it this morning. Crouching down to my knees, I bend over and guide it into the track.

"You need to screw it in," I say as I get up, trading places with Carson. "I don't want that thing falling over on us and making a mess."

He gets down on his hands and knees and leans over to fasten the screws into the base of the tree. I notice his shirt ride up and can't help but stare. But then a thought occurs to me: did he just do that to me when I was in that position?

Nope. Not going there. There will be no fornicating on this trip.

"There," he says with a sigh as he sits back on his heels. "I think that's good enough. You can let go."

I release my hold but keep my hands inches away just in case it starts to tip. But it just sits there, firmly in place.

"Perfect," I say. "Now the cleanup."

"Grab the broom and clean up these needles," he says. "I'll look out in the garage for the lights that Taylor says is out there." On his way out the door, he pulls away the prop on the door and closes it behind him, sealing in whatever heat is leftover.

I kick off my boots at the door and hang my hat, coat, and gloves on the rack by the door. Then I go to the closet behind the stairs and pull out the broom.

After a few minutes, I notice that most of the needles are sticking to the wet patches on the floor from the melted snow. So then I go to the kitchen and pull out paper towels and clean up the floor on my hands and knees. All in the name of Christmas warmth. This better be worth it.

Just as I'm finishing up, Carson comes back in holding a tangle of lights.

"Don't!" I point to him at the door. "Boots off! Right now."

He sighs and kicks them off, setting them carefully on the boot tray. "Better?"

"Much. I take it we need to untangle those?"

"If they even work." He pulls off his coat and then carries the wad of lights over to the nearest outlet. In a flash they all come alive. White lights that light up the room since the tree now covers one of the windows.

"This is going to be a sad looking tree with just lights on it," I say.

"You could go make a bag of popcorn and start stringing it. I'll untangle the lights."

"Deal." I hate untangling lights. I always get so frustrated and end up breaking them.

Ten minutes later, we're seated next to each other on the couch, both of us working carefully on our own separate tasks. I've never strung popcorn before, but I found a needle in the junk drawer in the kitchen, along with some thread and just started stabbing. It's not difficult, just tedious.

"So," I say after I notice the prolonged silence. "What made you get a rental by yourself for Christmas? Did your girlfriend dump you after you booked it?"

"Don't have a girlfriend," he says matter-of-factly. His tongue sticks out a little as he maneuvers the strand around. "And I told you, I only booked this two days ago."

"Oh. Right."

"No, I'm interested in purchasing a rental house myself," he goes on. "For an Airbnb, that is. I've stayed in quite a few, actually. Different ones. I've just never stayed in one around the holidays and it made me wonder how someone else handles that."

"Hmm." I wasn't buying that explanation. At least not completely. "And you decided to come by yourself because…?"

He shrugs. "No one to come with, I guess. What about you? How did you end up spending the holidays alone in a rental?"

Because I'm about to get fired and wanted to leave town before that could happen and ruin my Christmas, I think to myself. But the truth would require further details that I didn't want to get into.

"You're going to laugh," I say instead.

"Steph, you already make me laugh," he says. "How much worse can it get?"

I roll my eyes. "Okay. Fine. I was sitting at home, watching Hallmark movies and I saw the perfect small town Christmas settings that the stories would take place in and I—I don't know." I shrug. "I guess I just wanted to have a picturesque Christmas for once."

"So a movie brought you here?"

I nod. "I guess so."

"And you didn't bring your boyfriend along?"

He's fishing for information, I think to myself. *Is he flirting? No. Carson isn't interested in me like that. He doesn't even know me.*

"None to take," I say. "My husband might wonder where I am, though."

He looks up from his work. "You're married?"

I smile. "That was a joke."

Slowly, a grin stretches across his face. "Oh. Right. Clever." He splays out the strand. "I think these are mostly untangled."

"Not fair! I thought stringing the popcorn would be the easy job!"

He offers a devilish grin. "You've never done it before, have you?"

"Is it that obvious?"

"Only because you didn't object." His look softens and he adds, "Here, hand me a needle and thread and I'll help. We're going to need a lot. We have a huge tree."

"You're telling me!"

DECEMBER 19TH
Carson

❄ ❄ ❄

"Good morning!" Taylor beams at the door first thing in the morning.

Literally, I've made it as far as the bathroom and the bottom of the stairs since getting out of bed only a few minutes ago.

The cold air sweeps in the house as Taylor comes inside. She hands me a folded newspaper that's clearly already been read.

"This is for you," she says.

I put a finger to my lips and nod my head back toward Steph's bedroom. "She's still sleeping."

"Oh. Sorry. I just wanted to drop this off on my way in to work."

In the back of my mind, I vaguely remember that

today is Monday. Thankfully, I'm on vacation and that little detail doesn't really matter to me.

"I think it's a nice gesture to deliver the local newspaper to the house, but I don't want to subscribe to the house specifically," she says. "Not everyone reads the paper and I don't always have the house booked, so it'd be a waste."

Opening it, I peek inside at the headlines. "Thanks."

"There might not be anything in there that interests you, but there are some local activities that are listed. Sorry it's the Saturday paper, so it's a few days old. We get it first at our house and then I bring it here. The paper isn't published on Sundays or Mondays, so I guess this is still the latest copy."

I nod. "Okay. I'll check it out."

"How are things going? Everything okay?"

Ah, the real reason she came. "Not bad, actually. We've been getting along pretty well."

Taylor breathes a sigh of relief. "Oh good! I was kind of worried when I left you both on Saturday." She points to the tree by the window. "That looks nice. Did you go to get that together?"

"We did, yeah. It was fun. This trip might not be so bad."

She smiles. "I'm so happy about that. Well, I should be off. I don't want to intrude on your vacation anymore than I have to. Give me a call if you need anything. I only live five minutes away."

Just as quickly as she came, she's gone.

I make my way to the kitchen, fix myself a cup of coffee, and idly look over the newspaper while I wait for my cup to fill. In the "Lifestyles" section is a calendar list of events. One in particular catches my eye and I weigh my options.

We don't have anything planned for today, but isn't that the point of this vacation? Relaxation? Would Steph even be open to the idea of doing something with me? Would she be annoyed if I made plans for the two of us? Would she think there was some other intention behind it? Is there?

My coffee finishes brewing and I turn to retrieve the cup. It's nearly eight o'clock and Steph still isn't up yet. I decide to jump in the shower first so maybe I can enjoy breakfast with her.

I grab my cup of coffee and start to leave the room, but circle back and grab the newspaper. I want to give this some more thought. Maybe I can make the arrangements and surprise Steph. That wouldn't be terrible, would it?

DECEMBER 19TH
Carson

Should I be nervous about where you're taking me?" Steph asks as I lead her through the door.

"Two steps up," I tell her, using our clasped hands to guide her. "There you go, you got it."

"Carson, seriously."

I smile as she squeezes my hands tighter. There's a black blindfold over her eyes, which took a lot of convincing but she finally agreed to it.

"Just a few more steps."

She sighs audibly, but indulges me for a moment longer.

When we're finally through the doorway into the hall, I say, "Okay, now you can take it off."

Immediately, she pulls off the blindfold, but stops

and stares as the room comes into focus for her.

We're standing in the basement hall of one of the large churches on Main Street. The room smells of steamed vegetables and those heat canisters you use for graduation parties and summer cookouts. There are tables lined along was wall, where an assortment of food is being served by older women in white aprons with cutesy Christmas sweaters peeking out of the top.

"What is this?"

"This is your surprise," I say with a smile.

She raises her eyebrows and turns to me, but her eyes are still locked onto the crowd making its way along the tables. At the start of the row of tables are styrofoam to-go containers.

"It's a food drive," I explain. "I found out that every week this church provides meals for people who need it. Between Thanksgiving and Christmas, they serve three times a week."

"Uh-huh," she says slowly, still not following where this is going.

"In the paper that Taylor dropped off this morning, it said they were still looking for volunteers for today since a lot of their weekend volunteers work during the week," I go on. "So I signed us up."

"Oh."

"You don't sound very excited."

Steph still stares around before slowly peeling her eyes off the room and turning back to me. "No,

I'm just…I guess I'm still confused…"

Before I have a chance to reply, a woman from across the room calls to us. "Oh! Are you the volunteers?"

She has bright blonde hair, a huge smile, and the frilliest Christmas sweater out of everyone in the room. And, naturally, she's also wearing a Santa hat. Seems like the type of person who wears one the whole month of December.

"I'm just so excited that you're here!" she says as she steps toward us, still keeping her voice just as loud. "This is just such a great cause and I hate to see the rest of the volunteers struggle. If not enough people help, then we wouldn't be able to pull this off every year and the community really needs it."

"We're happy to help," Steph says.

The woman sticks out her hand abruptly in greeting. "I'm Daisy, I'm helping organize the drive this year."

We both introduce ourselves.

"It's so great when couples come to help us together," Daisy says. "We have Ethel and Arthur who come every year, right over there." She turns and waves to an elderly couple serving roast beef. "In the past, we've have Stanley and his wife Maggie, but he's really been slowing down in the last couple months so I didn't want to bother them. But I think it's great that you two are here! I wish I could drag my husband to these kinds of things, but that's a whole other issue."

"We're not—" I start.

"We're single," Steph blurts. "We're just, um…friends?" She looks to me for confirmation that the title fits our situation.

"New friends," I amend.

"*Very* new friends," Steph says.

Daisy looks between us as we sputter. Then she claps her hands together and says, "Well. Whatever you two are to each other, I'm glad you're here." She turns and waves us forward. "Come on. I need you in the kitchen."

We follow her, both of us probably wondering how exactly this is going to play out.

"We need one of you to bake the dinner rolls," Daisy explains. "They're real simple. Just pull them out of the freezer, set them on a pan, pop them in the oven—it should already be set to the right temperature—and keep them in there for about ten minutes until they turn golden. While one of you is doing that, the other can bring the dishes from the window and over to the sink so Betty can put them in the dishwasher. Any questions?"

I shake my head and turn to Steph.

"Where are the aprons?" she asks.

"Oh dear! I completely forgot! They're right behind the door, honey. Help yourself."

Steph walks over and gets one for each of us. These things were probably once white, but they'd been stained and washed so many times that they had a gray hue to them.

"Thank you both so much," Daisy says again. "I'll be in and out if you need anything. The next shift comes in at two, so you have a few hours! Oh, and help yourself to a plate when you're done! Good luck!"

Like a hurricane, Daisy left, leaving us both a little dazed.

"I can take the dishes," I offer.

"No, I've got them," Steph says. "You can handle the rolls. Ovens scare me."

"Scare you?" I ask as I pull the bag of rolls out of the freezer. They're simple ready-to-make ones that you find at the discount section of the grocery store. "How do ovens scare you?"

"They're hot." She carries a stack of dishes in a plastic bin around the corner to the sink near the dishwasher. When she comes back around, she adds, "I don't like sticking my hands in anything hot."

"That's why they make oven mitts."

"Still freaks me out."

"Let me guess, you burned yourself on the oven as a kid?"

"Those things are dangerous!"

"And necessary," I say with a laugh. With the pan filled, I open the oven door and feel a wave of heat escape. To myself, I admit that Steph may be onto something here. The oven *is* really hot.

"So what made you sign us up for this?" she asks as she stacks more dirty dishes into the bin.

"You said you wanted to experience a small town Christmas," I say. "So I figured what better way to do that than to see the community at its best, by helping its neighbors. I didn't think Daisy would stick us in the back out of sight, though."

"Well, we're newbies, and we aren't *really* a part of the community, so maybe that's what she's thinking. But it was still a sweet idea."

"Wasn't it?"

She rolls her eyes as she walks by me. "And you're so humble about it too."

I laugh. "I just wanted to do something nice for you. I still feel a little guilty for crashing your Christmas."

"You're not crashing my Christmas," she says. "Not anymore, at least."

"Were you planning on family coming to stay with you?"

"Nope." She passes by on another trip to the dishwasher.

"You were just going to stay in that big house by yourself?"

"What about *your* family?" she fires back.

My mind fills with Grandpa and I crack a joke to defuse whatever feelings that start bubbling up. "My family doesn't even know you. Why would they plan a vacation with you?"

Another eye roll. "You know what I meant. Besides, my parents are visiting my brother in Seattle this year for Christmas. And even if they weren't, they live in Maine, so no, they're not coming to stay with me out here."

"Why didn't you go to Seattle with them?"

She shrugs as she turns her back to load up the dishes into the bin. "I don't know. Lots of reasons, I guess. Time off work, no money, my brother's apartment is kind of small. It was just easier to stay here."

The timer dings. I open the oven door, pull out the pan, and set it on the stovetop burners. "But it's Christmas. Isn't that when you're supposed to get uncomfortably close with your family?"

"I just didn't go, okay?" she snaps. The tone of her voice says that the conversation is officially over and she will not entertain anymore questions.

"Well," I say, putting a better end to the topic. "The two of us will have to have our own uncomfortable Christmas this year, then."

DECEMBER 20TH
Steph

***

The microwave dings and the smell of popcorn fills the chilly kitchen. My toes are cold, even in my fuzzy socks. I finish stirring my hot chocolate, adding in a peppermint candy for extra flavor, and go over to the microwave to retrieve my popcorn.

With snacks in hand, I make my way back to the living room to settle on the oversized couch. My plan is to watch Christmas movies all day. It's really the only option for such a snowy day. Besides, Carson and I spent most of yesterday helping perfect strangers, so I don't feel guilty to self-indulge today.

"I smell popcorn," Carson says as he comes down the stairs. Old Spice body wash wafts behind him as he disappears into the kitchen.

"I'm taking on the classics today," I tell him.

"And the classics would be...?" he asks as he comes back in with a cup of coffee. He steps right behind the couch and I crane my neck to look up at him.

"The plan is to start with *White Christmas*, then *Miracle on 34th Street*—the original. We can watch the 90s remake later this week if you insist—and then we'll go from there."

"Throw in *It's a Wonderful Life* and I'm in," Carson says without hesitation. "Are you going to share your popcorn or should I make my own?"

"Hmm," I study him, guarding the bowl protectively. "I suppose I can share a little. But if we need a refill, you're making it."

"Sounds good." He comes around and sits on the other end of the couch. With his long arms, he can reach the bowl if I set it beside me. He just needs to lean over a little bit.

I scroll through the streaming options and find the Bing Crosby classic. "You ready?"

Carson rubs his hands together. "Oh, I'm ready! My grandfather used to force me to watch this as a kid. Well, this and *It's a Wonderful Life*. I used to think they were so boring because they were in black and white, but now I think they're an essential part of the holiday season."

"Hmm." I tap the remote against the tip of my nose, my thumb hovering over the "Play" button.

"What?" he asks.

"Just wondering if you're going to talk through the whole movie."

He laughs.

"Seriously, I'm considering withdrawing my offer to let you watch a movie with me," I say with my own smirk.

"You wouldn't leave me upstairs all on my own, would you?"

I shrug, loving this give and take we've developed. It's great to not have this situation be *totally* awkward.

"I'd be crying." He pushes his lower lip out into an exaggerated pout.

"I wouldn't be able to hear you over the movie," I add.

He laughs again. "So cold! Okay, I can take a hint. I'll be quiet."

"Good." I point the remote at the TV and start the movie.

Everything starts off fine. I'm enjoying the movie, not thinking about much else, completely relaxing…and then my hand brushes against Carson's in the popcorn bowl.

Total cliché, I know. But it gets my mind on the possibility of being close with Carson. Like…*intimately* close.

It's really the first time that I've even thought about it. And it's obviously just a fantasy, but it's something that's on my mind for the duration of the movie. How Carson has seen me naked, even before we knew each other's names. How we've been spending so much time together. How easily we've fallen into our own unique routine in this weird situation.

Just as *White Christmas* is wrapping up, my mind is consumed with the possibility that maybe Carson *wasn't* joking the other day when he offered to have me sneak a peek when he was in the shower. Maybe he's pushing for something to happen between us and I'm just blind to it. Maybe he thinks—

"More popcorn?" he asks, abruptly pulling me out of my head.

"Huh?" My eyes flicker up and I see the credits roll. I reach over for the remote and go back to the main menu. "Uh, sure. Yeah."

"Did you fall asleep?" he asks as he takes the bowl across into the kitchen.

I throw back the blanket and grab our empty mugs and follow him into the next room. "Not quite. Just relaxing, that's all. It's what I've needed, honestly."

"Me too," he says. "Glad we have this distraction." He sets a new bag of popcorn in the microwave and starts it.

"Refill?" I raise the mug in a question.

"Sure, why not?"

Over at the Keurig, I reach for another K-cup of

hot chocolate, but there's only one. Searching through the cupboards nearby, I can't seem to locate them. "Didn't Taylor say there's a pantry around here?"

"Over here." Carson opens the large cupboard beside the fridge and finds the box of K-cups. He pulls them out and then stops. "Whoa, what do we have here?"

"What?" I ask, consciously keeping my distance across the room. Afraid that he somehow knows the thoughts that have been floating in my head during the movie. Stupid, I know, but it's enough to make me tread carefully with him.

He bends down and retrieves something from the bottom of the pantry. "You want to add a little cream to your hot chocolate?"

I make a face, my mind immediately going in the gutter.

"Taylor's got Irish cream here! It's a Bailey's knock-off, but it'll work."

"Is it even any good?" I ask.

"Seals not even broken." He brings it over and screws off the top, pouring a liberal amount to his own mug.

I look at him with raised eyebrows.

"What?" He shrugs. "It's not like I'm going anywhere."

"True." I set the first mug in place and start the Keurig, just as Carson goes to retrieve the popcorn.

"So is this your holiday tradition? Do you belong to one of those families who just gets drunk on Christmas Eve and wakes up the next morning feeling hungover and miserable?"

"Nah, my grandpa wasn't much of a drinker. During the holidays he made the exception, but even then it wasn't too much."

I nod and replace the mug, starting the machine for the second cup.

"What about you?" he asks.

"My parents—my *mother*—isn't a fan of 'the drink,' as she calls it," I say. "I went through a phase in my early twenties when that was basically all I did every weekend, but I quickly got over it. Now, it's just special occasions."

"Well, today must be a special occasion." He pops one kernel of popcorn in his mouth and grins just before he escapes back into the living room.

When my hot chocolate is finished brewing, I open the Irish cream and pour a good amount into my mug. For good measure, I take a deep swig straight from the bottle, feeling the warmth burn all over.

Carrying the cups back into the living room, I gather my courage and say something that Carson would only respond positively to if he really is trying to come on to me.

"You know," I start. "Even though I wasn't happy about it at first, I'm actually glad you're here."

"Yeah?" he asks with a smirk.

"I don't think this would be nearly as much fun if I didn't have someone to pick on the whole time."

He laughs. "Oh, so I'm just your punching bag?"

I shrug.

"Well, then maybe I won't share my popcorn."

"Then maybe I won't share the blanket."

"You didn't during the first movie."

"Maybe I've changed my mind since then," I tell him.

"I could use it. It's pretty chilly in here."

I roll my eyes playfully and toss some of the blanket over to him. "Just don't get fresh with me."

"Wouldn't dream of it."

And, as we settle in to watch our second movie, I spend the duration dissecting every interaction we've ever had.

DECEMBER 21ST
Carson

I catch myself whistling along to the radio—which is playing "All I Want For Christmas Is You" by Mariah Carey—as I make breakfast for me and Steph. The eggs are finishing up in the pan, the cinnamon rolls are ready to come out of the oven, and the bacon has already been fried. It's probably the world's most unhealthiest breakfast, but hey, we're on vacation.

Last night, Steph was different. She seemed to be distant and yet interested in me all at the same time. Like she was nervous or something. To make things even more confusing, I had a dream that the two of us were celebrating Christmas together. As a couple. Of course, that's probably because by the end of the third movie last night, we were practically laying on each other.

It first started as a joke. I had put my leg up on her as I stretched out in an exaggerated way. To my surprise, she grabbed my leg and made a comment about how firm everything felt. Next thing I knew, we were comparing the size of each other's calves. As we settled back into the movie, she had put her legs over my lap and my hand was casually resting just above her knee.

Then, after the movie, it was off to bed without much more than a "Good night" between us. But still, something has shifted in our convoluted relationship. And making breakfast is a good way to start the conversation about where this could go.

Steph enters the kitchen just as I'm distributing the food onto the plates. She's still in her pajamas: red and black plaid pants, a hoodie, and wool socks on her feet. Her hair is piled on top of her head in a frizzy, messy bun that has long since deflated.

"Could you clang any louder?" she asks.

"Sorry. Did I wake you up?"

"Between the dishes and the music and the smell of grease, it was hard to sleep in," she says. "And did I tell you how much I hate whistling?"

Didn't even realize I was still doing it. Immediately, I stop. "Maybe this will cheer you up." I bring over our full plates to the table, where she's sitting. "Full course breakfast!"

"Thanks," she mutters quietly.

"How'd you sleep?" I ask.

"Fine."

"Not too tired after last night's indulgence?"

"No."

"I thought yesterday was fun." I can hear how painfully obvious it is that Steph doesn't want to converse, but still I proceed. "And the snow seems to have stopped. The sun is nearly blinding with the white—"

"Could you stop?" she snaps. "I don't care about the weather."

Hint taken. I turn my head down to my plate and stab at my eggs, frustrated at the mixed signals. Yesterday she seemed to want to get closer to me and yet today she acts like I'm the scum of the earth. What gives? Did she think over what happened last night? Does she regret what happened between us? Not that *anything* really happened. We broke the barrier of touch, which is about the extent of anything romantic. To use the outdated teenaged terminology, that's not even first base!

Fine. If Steph doesn't want anything to happen between us, then nothing will happen between us. It's not like I'm on this trip to find a girlfriend or anything. I just needed—

"Sorry," she says, breaking into my thoughts. "I'm in a bad mood."

"I gathered that."

"The truth is, I'm on this trip as an escape."

"An escape?"

She picks up her toast and tears at the corner, popping small pieces in her mouth. "From work stuff."

"Oh. But why the sudden mood swing?"

"I thought I'd check in on my work email this morning, which was a mistake."

"Bad news?"

"I read something that annoyed me."

Turning back to my food, I shrug. "Just ignore it. You're on vacation. It can wait until—"

"I *can't* ignore it," she cuts in. "This is *my job*. The thing that pays the bills. And thanks to a jerk, I probably won't even have a job to go back to."

"You're getting fired?"

"No," she snaps, then a moment later adds, "Possibly. Maybe. I don't know. It's not good."

"And you thought this was the perfect time to go on a vacation?" As soon as the words slip out of my mouth, I know they're a mistake.

Steph's glaring look confirms my thoughts. "Do you have something to say about the way I live my life?"

In an effort to diffuse the situation, I turn back to my food and shove a mouthful in, not really tasting it. When I finish that bite, I say, "Nothing. Forget I said anything."

"But you did say it," she pushes.

"Just try to relax," I murmur. "That's all I'm saying."